To my grandson.
May all your Christmas
wishes come true!

Love.................................

I am so *excited*
Christmastime is here!

"I really wish for lots and lots of fluffy snow this year!"

I sit and write to Santa.
The letter takes me ages.

"Perhaps I've wished for way too much?"
(There are over 50 pages!)

I help to decorate the tree
with twinkly lights that glow.

Christmas
decorations

Look at me! I'm up on stage,
and in the Christmas play.

I wished to make
my family proud,
and have the greatest day!

The kitchen's very busy.
I smell the cookies baking.

I run downstairs
to find a pile of
presents beneath
the tree.

Love
Santa

This sweater's really **itchy**.
I try to grin and bear it,
but what I really wish is that
I didn't have to wear it!

I am very happy—
my wish for snow came true!

I'm off to build a snowman now.
Perhaps I will build two!

I go sledding
with my friends.
"I wish I could
speed up!"

My wish comes true,
my sled is *fast*
when powered by a pup!

It's after Christmas dinner,
and everyone is snoring.
I yawn and say to my best friend,
"I wish it was less **BORING!**"

Mom holds my hands and asks me,
"Did your **BIGGEST** wish come true?"
"Oh yes," I smile,
"that wish was being..."

"...here with **all** of you!"

Do you wish for fun with friends,
or a family trip that never ends?
Whatever it is that you hold dear,
keep your Christmas wishes here!

I wish...

Published by Put Me In The Story,
a publication of Sourcebooks, Inc.
P.O. Box 4410, Naperville, Illinois 60567-4410
(630) 961-3900
Fax: (630) 961-2168
www.putmeinthestory.com

Date of Production: August 2018
Run Number: HTW_PO201829
Printed and bound in China (GD)
10 9 8 7 6 5 4 3 2 1